2014

You Can't Walk a Fish!

A Matthew McFarland Series Book

Book 2

Lisa Funari Willever

Illustrated by
Glenn Byrne
and
Elaine Poller

Special Guest Young Author & Illustrator Section

We Support

the four foundation

Franklin Mason Press

Trenton, New Jersey

To my dear friend, Suzanne Rhoads, who probably could walk a fish if she put her mind to it.
Enjoy Molly…**LFW**

To the new love in my life, little Rebecca...and to the original, my husband, Bradley...
thanks for giving me the best of everything…**EP**

To my mother, the strongest woman on earth. Thank you for putting my doodles on the fridge.
I love you…**Glenn**

The editors of Franklin Mason Press would like to thank those who graciously serve on the Guest Young Author and Guest Young Illustrator committees. Your care in selecting the work of young writers and artists today will help to shape and inspire the authors and illustrators of tomorrow.

Text copyright © Lisa Funari Willever, 2003
Illustration copyright © Elaine Poller and Glenn Byrne, 2003
Editorial Staff – Marcia Jacobs, Linda Funari, Catherine Funari
Cover and Interior Design – Peri Poloni, Knockout Design, www.knockoutbooks.com

Published in the United States – Printed in Singapore
Franklin Mason Press
ISBN No. 0-9679227-1-2
Library of Congress Control Number – 2002095002
10 9 8 7 6 5 4 3 2

Other Franklin Mason Press Titles
Everybody Moos At Cows
Where Do Snowmen Go?
Chumpkin
The Easter Chicken
Maximilian The Great
On Your Mark, Get Set, Teach!

the four foundation

Franklin Mason Press is proud to support the important work of The Four Foundation.
In that spirit, $0.25 will be donated from the sale of each book. To learn more about their work,
see our About The Charity Page at the end of the book or visit www.franklinmasonpress.com.

Today, I think that I will ask my mother and my father, if I can have a puppy, though I don't know why I bother.

"OLDER"

MAtt
―――
AGE 5

MAtt
―――
AGE 3

MAtt
―――
AGE 1

Time and time again I ask, "When will I have this pet?"
They say, "When you are older, Matt," and hope that I'll forget.

"**I**t's a big responsibility," my parents, they insist.

So I try hard to look mature and carefully persist.

Since I was two,

I always knew

I'd have to have a puppy.

So imagine my surprise

when dad said,

"How about a GUPPY?"

guppy is no puppy! They must know that it's a fish!

I was hoping he was joking, but I didn't get my wish.

He said, "You've made it crystal clear, you'd like another pet.

But a puppy is a lot of work and you're not ready yet."

Plan A had quickly crumbled, it completely fell apart.

Plan B would work for sure, for it was touching, it was smart.

The Johnson's down the street, you know, they have a situation.

They need someone to watch their dog, when they go on vacation.

'd be helping out the Johnson's as I watch their brand-new puppy.

I would prove I was responsible and they'd forget the guppy!

I'd teach her all the tricks that I've been storing in my head.

I'd have her sitting up,

rolling over,

playing dead.

I'd give her biscuits, give her bones, whatever she may like.

Maybe I could teach her how to ride a little bike.

I had big plans for this puppy, there'd be big fun everyday.

I couldn't wait to meet her, so I took off right away.

Mrs. Johnson said she'd pay me

for my time and for my trouble.

If I knew then, what I know now,

I would have charged her double.

had heard about big puppies, but I never thought I'd meet...

a puppy that was bigger than some cars parked on the street.

Puddles was a sheepdog and she was quite a sight.

I only hoped her hearty bark was much worse than her bite.

She started coming towards us, it was too late to retreat.

Puddles jumped up on my shoulders. Puddles knocked me off my feet.

As I lay in Mrs. Johnson's yard, the victim in this game.

I felt a puddle on my shirt and knew how Puddles got her name.

"**S**ometimes she gets excited," Mrs. Johnson started saying.

"She's only just a puppy, she's really only playing."

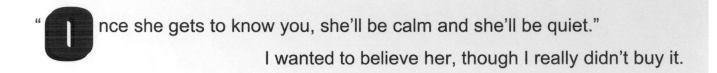

"Once she gets to know you, she'll be calm and she'll be quiet."

I wanted to believe her, though I really didn't buy it.

But I had made a promise

and I am not a quitter.

It was clear that for

the next two weeks,

I'd be a

MONSTER SITTER!

She barked and barked for hours. The mailman she would stalk.

And when I held her giant leash...she took ME for a walk!

She ate the biscuits, ate the bones, whatever she could munch.

Forget about the bike...she would have eaten it for lunch!

She ate the cushions from the couch, each time she was alone.

Nothing in the house was safe, she even ate the phone!

One week spent with Puddles, while it wasn't what I'd wished,
convinced me that my dad was right and I should try a fish.

A fish was not so bad, I thought. In fact, it could be great.

I'd buy a fishbowl and some stones. I really couldn't wait.

So what if I can't walk my fish, I am not complaining.

It's better looking through the glass, especially when its raining!

Guest Young Author

First Place – **Ceili Burdhimo Age 8**
H. Russell Swift Elementary School — Egg Harbor Twp, New Jersey

The Cats Who Thought They Were Human

One day, two cats named Pumpkin and Noel saw their owners playing charades. One of the owners was acting like a cat, crawling on the floor and meowing. The other owner laughed. It was so funny, everyone else started acting like cats. Since the owners were acting like cats, the cats thought that they should act like humans.

The first human thing they thought they should do was to take a shower. When the owners went to the movies, the cats snuck into the shower. At first they did not like it, but they got used to it. When the owners came home, they wondered why the cats were all wet.

When it was their feeding time, Noel did not want to eat like a cat. Instead she used her paws. Pumpkin tried to walk on her hind legs. At first she fell, then she got the hang of it. One day, the cats started watching TV. They saw a cat on the TV and thought he was in the same room, so they started talking to him.

The owners like when their cats try to act like humans, even when they are bad, because it makes them laugh. Laughing makes people happy and the cats bring happiness to their owners.

Second Place –
Rebecca Smith   Age 6
Veterans Memorial Elementary School
Brick, New Jersey

The Dog That Changes Colors

Cindy has a little white dog, named Skippy. On Monday, Cindy took Skippy for a walk. He loved going for a walk and he turned pink because he was happy.

On Tuesday, Cindy went shopping with her mom. Skippy was all alone at home. Skippy didn't like to be alone and he turned blue because he was sad.

On Wednesday, Cindy's little brother took Skippy's favorite bone. Skippy turned red because he was mad.

On Thursday, Cindy pet the neighbor's dog and Skippy turned green because he was jealous.

On Friday, Cindy said, "Skippy, it doesn't matter what color you are. I love you because you are the best dog."

Third Place –
Jenna Postiglione   Age 6
Millstone Elementary School
Millstone, New Jersey

A New Friend

Once upon a time, there was a lonely toad named JuJu. She had no friends. She did have a boat that could not float. One day she decided to leave the boat on the side of the road with a note. The note said, "Dear God, I don't need a boat that doesn't float. Can you find somebody who does? Thank you."

When she came back, the boat was gone. In its place there was a dog with a bone. Around his neck was soap on a rope. On the soap it said, "I knew you could not use a boat that doesn't float, so I left you a friend instead. Love, God."

Guest Young Illustrator

First Place –
Colin Slusher Age 9
Seaview Avenue
Elementary School
Linwood, New Jersey

"You Can Walk A Fish"

Second Place –
Alexander Torgeson Age 8
Waxhaw Elementary School
Waxhaw, North Carolina

"Before Cell Phones"

Third Place – Tie
Maureen Mullins   Age 9
University Heights Elementary School
Mercerville, New Jersey

"Dolphin Dance"

Third Place – Tie
Billy Grant   Age 7
H. Russell Swift School
Egg Harbor Twp, New Jersey

"As Freedom Waves"

Would You Like To Be An Author or Illustrator?

Franklin Mason Press is looking for stories and illustrations from children 6-9 years old to appear in our books. We are dedicated to providing children with an avenue into the world of publishing.

If you would like to be our next Guest Young Author or Guest Young Illustrator, read the information below and send us your work.

To be a Guest Young Author:

Send us a 75-200 word story about something strange, funny, or unusual. Stories may be fiction or non-fiction. Be sure to follow the rules below.

To be a Guest Young Illustrator:

Draw a picture using crayons, markers, or colored pencils. Do not write words on your picture and be sure to follow the rules below.

Prizes

1st Place Author / 1st Place Illustrator

$25.00, a framed award, a complimentary book and your work will be published in FMP's newest book.

2nd Place Author / 2nd Place Illustrator

$15.00, a framed award, a complimentary book and your work will be published in FMP's newest book.

3rd Place Author / 3rd Place Illustrator

$10.00, a framed award, a complimentary book and your work will be published in FMP's newest book.

Rules For The Contest

1. Children may enter one category only, either Author or Illustrator.
2. All stories must be typed or written very neatly.
3. All illustrations must be sent in between 2 pieces of cardboard to prevent wrinkling.
4. Name, age, address, phone number, school, and parent's signature must be on the back of all submissions.
5. All work must be original and completed solely by the child.
6. Franklin Mason Press reserves the right to print submitted material. All work becomes property of FMP and will not be returned. Any work selected is considered a work for hire and FMP will retain all rights.
7. There is no deadline for submissions. FMP will publish children's work in every book published. All submissions are considered for the most current title.
8. All submissions should be sent to:

Youth Submissions Editor
Franklin Mason Press
P. O. Box 3808
Trenton, NJ 08629
www.franklinmasonpress.com

Franklin Mason Press is proud to donate twenty-five cents, from the sale of each copy of *You Can't Walk a Fish*, to the Four Foundation. Below, we have provided information about their valuable work in the area of pediatric brain tumors. We are honored to play a role in their important mission.

The Four Foundation was founded for the purpose of assisting researchers at Columbia-Presbyterian Medical Center in developing new and successful treatments for children stricken with brain tumors, as well as to increase the cure rate for these children and to spare them and their parents the anguish of such a horrible illness. Current treatments allow only for the medicine and technology of the past. Treatment of brain tumors has not substantially advanced in decades. Only with research can there be hope for the future. Only with research can children have a fighting chance to overcome their brain tumors with complete confidence.

The Four Foundation's driving commitment is fueled with desire and pledged to, "Whoever saves one life, saves the world entire."

**Four Foundation — 173 Pascack Avenue, Emerson, NJ 07630
201-265-8440—tarallo@fourfoundation.org**

About the Author & Illustrators

Lisa Funari Willever (author) is a lifelong resident of Trenton, New Jersey and a former fourth grade teacher. She is a graduate of The College of New Jersey and a member of the National Education Association, the New Jersey Education Association, and the New Jersey Reading *Association*. Lisa is the author of *The Culprit Was A Fly, Miracle On Theodore's Street, Maximilian The Great, The Easter Chicken, Chumpkin, Everybody Moos At Cows, Where Do Snowmen Go,* and *On Your Mark, Get Set, Teach.* Her husband, Todd is a professional firefighter in the city of Trenton and the co-author of *Miracle On Theodore's Street.* They are the proud parents of three year old, Jessica Marie and two year old, Patrick Timothy.

Elaine Poller (illustrator) started drawing at age three. Her first drawings were of a family of characters called "Eekies". Elaine graduated from The College of New Jersey, where she earned a BFA in Graphic Design with a minor in illustration. She currently works in New York City as a clothing designer for children, but believes her greatest creation yet is her new baby girl, Rebecca Paige. She resides in Edgewater, New Jersey with Rebecca and husband, Bradley. This is her second children's book.

When **Glenn Byrne** (illustrator) was 5 years old, he sold a drawing of a fire truck for one dollar. He decided this was a pretty cool way to make a buck. With much practice, he graduated with a BFA in Illustration at the Fashion Institute of Technology in New York City. There he met his wife, Michele, who currently works for a children's apparel company in Manhattan. They are the proud parents of McKenna Marie who just turned three. He helped illustrate *Everybody Moos at Cows* and this is his second children's book.